Princess Scallywag and the Brave, Brave Knight

MARK SPERRING

illustrated by

CLAIRE POWELL

HarperCollins *Children's Books*

One morning, the Queen looked out of her window and saw two things …

The first thing she saw was the kingdom's bravest knight skipping across the drawbridge.

And the second thing she saw was …

a BIG, BOTHERSOME... dragon!

"You down there!" called the Queen to the knight.

"If you rid this land of that **bothersome dragon**, you'll win the hand of my **delightful** daughter, Princess Scallywag."

"Me, marry the princess?!" spluttered the knight. "I couldn't **possibly** do that ...

I've heard she takes baths
in the moat with the
frogs and the toads!"

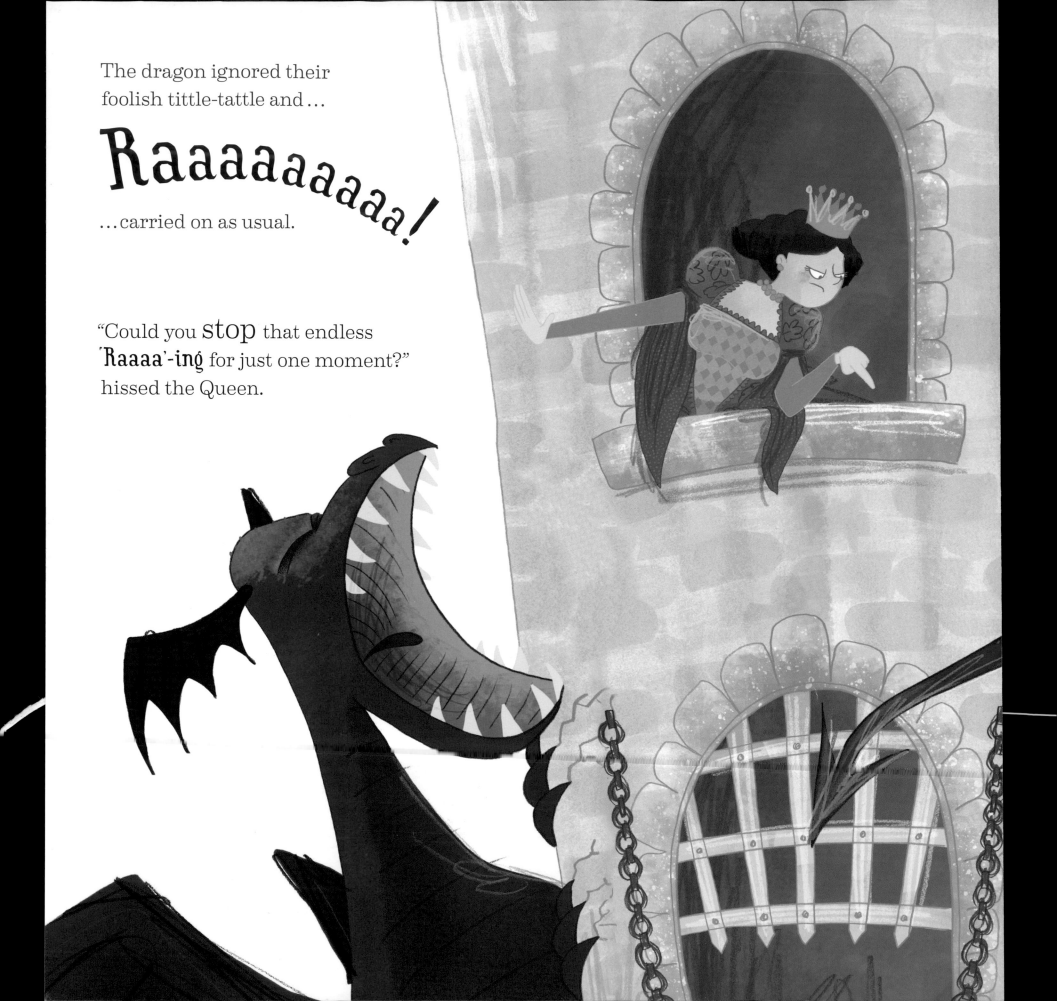

The dragon ignored their foolish tittle-tattle and...

Raaaaaaaaa!

...carried on as usual.

"Could you **stop** that endless 'Raaaa'-ing for just one moment?" hissed the Queen.

"But it's only fair you marry Princess Scallywag," she said. "If you save the kingdom, you marry the princess. It happens in all the stories all the time – don't you know?"

"I do know," said the knight, "but unfortunately, I've heard …

your daughter's feet smell like two slabs of **mouldy old** cheese!"

"Mere rumour!" sniffed the Queen with a wave of her hanky, and she carried on with the marriage plans regardless.

"So ... after you've done you-know-what to you-know-who ...

PRINCESS BRIDE

we'll boil up his bones, pickle his scales, and roast his toes over a nice, warm fire. Then we'll serve him up on a bed of chopped tomatoes and green lettuce leaves which will be perfect for the wedding feast!"

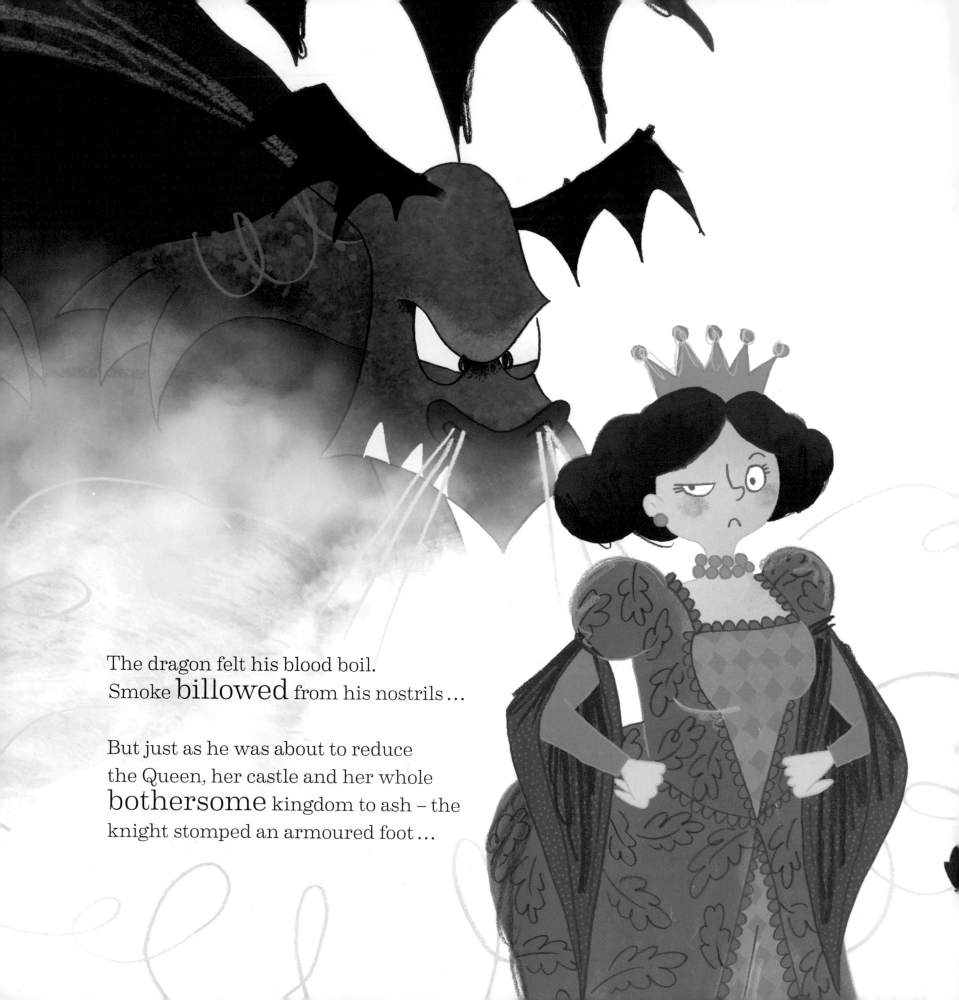

The dragon felt his blood boil.
Smoke billowed from his nostrils...

But just as he was about to reduce
the Queen, her castle and her whole
bothersome kingdom to ash – the
knight stomped an armoured foot...

"Seriously," said the knight, "I really couldn't possibly marry Princess Scallywag! You see …

I've heard she flies her grubby old knickers from the top of the flagpole!"

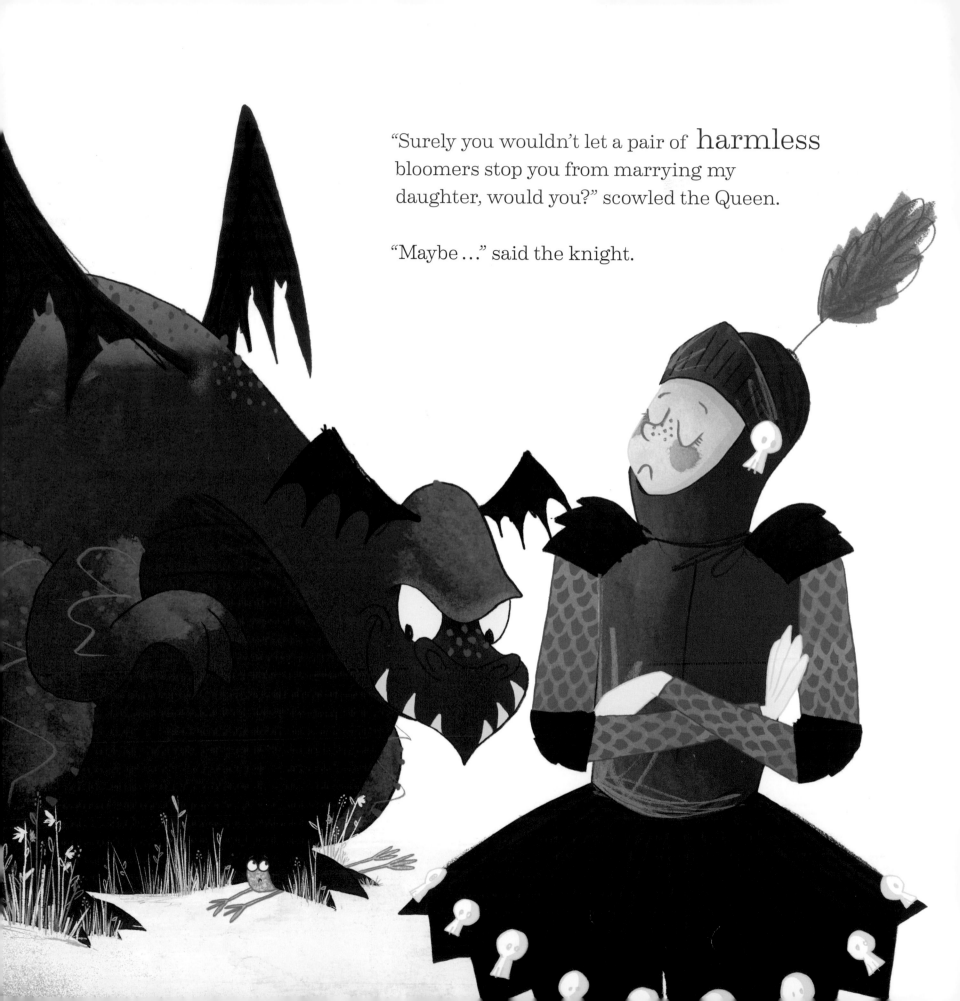

"Surely you wouldn't let a pair of **harmless** bloomers stop you from marrying my daughter, would you?" scowled the Queen.

"Maybe…" said the knight.

"Well I'm not having **this** story end without Princess Scallywag getting married and living

Happily
Ever After!

So... **you'll** just have to marry her!" said the Queen, pointing **pointedly** at ...

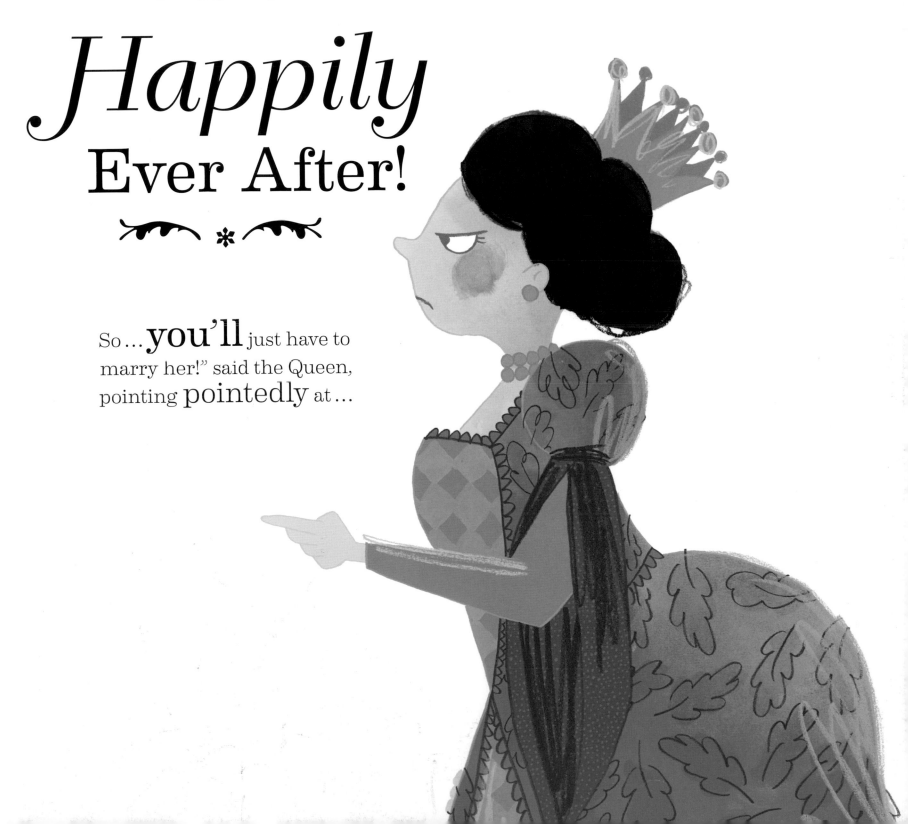

the **dragon!**

"Me?" gasped the dragon,
suddenly looking flustered.
"But I've only come here to burn
down the **entire** kingdom!"

"No excuses!" said the Queen.

"Princess Scallywag," she called,
"a lovely dragon **actually**
wants to marry you, so come
out now and show yourself,
before he changes
his mind and …

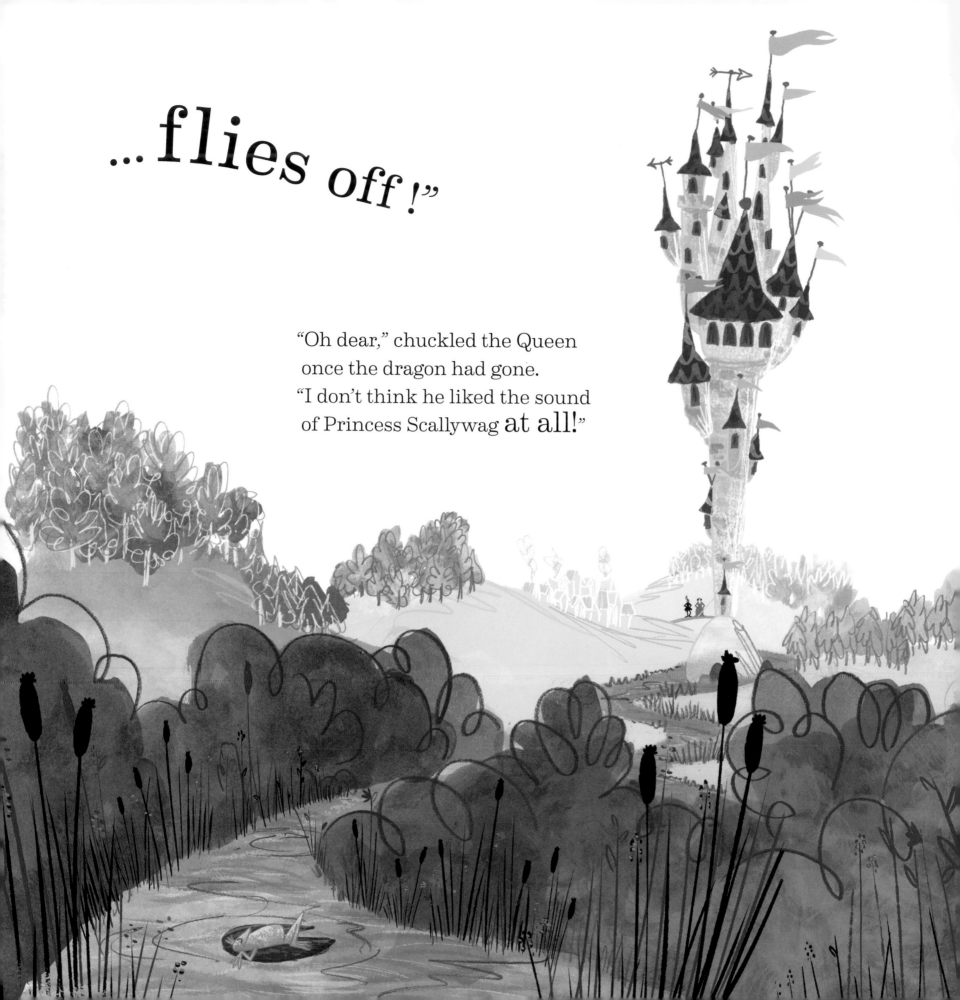

...flies off!"

"Oh dear," chuckled the Queen
once the dragon had gone.
"I don't think he liked the sound
of Princess Scallywag at all!"

"They **never** do!" laughed
Princess Scallywag,
throwing off her armour
with a triumphant

Clunk!

"But we always have
such **fun** getting
rid of them!"

"But how will we live

Happily Ever After

now?" giggled the Queen.

"Well …" said Princess Scallywag,
"we could always carry on doing
just what we've always done!"

"One problem …"
shrugged the Queen,
"we've scared away **every**
single dragon in the land!"

"Then we'll just have to move on to **BIGGER** and BETTER THINGS…" grinned Princess Scallywag.

And later that afternoon…

THUMP!

SHUDDER!

Grrrr!

...that's
EXACTLY
what they did!